The Hatanii Bride

Painted Wings Publishing

The Story Behind The Story

The Hatanii Bride is loosely inspired by the Polish fairy tale *O królewiczu Niespodzianku (The Unlooked-for Prince)*. Many readers and authors enjoy a good fairy tale retelling, so I perused several to find one to tackle. I came to realize just how misogynistic most tales are. In this particular tale, a prince is saved repeatedly by a woman with magic. That's awesome—a woman that's strong. But … it's not an equal partnership. And the only reason he won her eternal gratitude to get out of his mess? He did the bare minimum of giving back a dress he'd taken so she wouldn't be naked, and he called her pretty.

The tale is certainly not the worst out there (there's even talking spittle, which is a new one for me, so it's interesting and worth a read), but I wanted to put my own spin on it. That said, *The Hatanii Bride* doesn't much resemble the original, but there are nods to it. I liked the magical aspects and the fact that there were tasks to be completed. Instead of a story where one partner has to complete tasks and ends up winning their partner, why not have them face tasks together? Even better, why not have them complete those tasks to try to get away from each other in an enemies-to-lovers arranged marriage?

Unfortunately, the talking spittle did not get a cameo in *The Hatanii Bride,* but I hope you still enjoy it!

*

Sign up for my newsletter to get updates on upcoming publications, promotions, and bonus content! (Including a FREE download of "Son & Soldier: A Seeder Short Story" at JHouserWrites.com)

~Read bonus scenes from the love interest's perspective!~

Book-related merch can also be purchased on my author website!

The Hatanii Bride

J. HOUSER

Painted Wings Publishing

Chapter One

A trickle of sweat ran down Talia's back as she worked under the beating sun. She was careful to keep any sweat out of her eyes and project by tying up her long curly black hair with a wide band. She was careful, even intentional, about *everything* she was doing today.

Talia Mehaven had spent her entire childhood in the same home. A home built by her parents when they'd wed, when they'd participated in the hatanii ceremony. Hatanii was important to their people, a carefully planned marriage arrangement organized by the kingdom's elders. If you desired to wed, you participated in hatanii.

On completion of Talia's celebration of adulthood, her island's local elders had inquired of her and her parents if she was ready. Most people participated young, when they'd reached their eighteenth, nineteenth, or twentieth year. Her mother had been eighteen, her father nineteen at the time of their hatanii.

Today, Talia prepared for her own ceremony. *This would be much smoother if I could use magik.* She grumbled only a little at the parameters of the task at hand.

Preparations for hatanii were almost as rigorous as the ceremony itself. The bond was for life, not to be taken lightly. She'd already completed a thorough interview with her island elders, and her parents had been interviewed as well. Her magik, knowledge, and temperament had been tested.

Talia smiled as she slowly poured a bucket of rainwater and ash into a sieve, separating out the lye. She'd been matched. She didn't know who she'd matched with, or if he even lived on her island, but she'd been matched. And this batch of soap was for him.

Hatanii lasted a month, mostly held in seclusion while the couple got to know each other. As Talia was not an eldest child, due to inherit the family home, and apparently her betrothed wasn't either, their primary hatanii task would be building a home together.

Before the official ceremony, the bride and groom were tasked with preparing gifts for their betrothed. They had to be handmade—without magik—and should include something to enhance their future home, some type of adornment for their betrothed, and something practical that could be used before and during the hatanii ceremony.

With the lye now separate, Talia measured what she needed, minding the ratio of oils to lye to make perfect soap bars. She'd learned this skill from her mother at a young age, though she wasn't used to doing it all manually.

"How is it coming along?" her mother asked from behind.

"Ayo," Talia muttered. "Slow."

Her mother appeared on her left, glancing at the worktable. "Things that are worthwhile are worth taking time on."

Talia's lip twitched. "It might be better quality if magik was allowed for the gifts. And the homes sturdier if it was allowed for more of the ceremony."

Clasping her hands in front of her cobalt blue dress, her mother leaned against a palm tree, the fronds rustling ever so slightly in the breeze. "Our home *is* sturdy. And it's a reminder that we are more than magik, that we are equal with our match no matter our specialties, and that worthwhile things ought not to have shortcuts taken on them." Her mother paused. "You *do* want this, right?"

"Yes, I'm ready for it." Talia shook her head. "This part of it just seems silly."

Her mother's voice was soft, playful. "Do you think your betrothed grumbles over making *your* gifts?"

Talia couldn't help but smile at that. He was out there—whoever he was—thoughtfully making things for her too. "Only if he has half a brain," she kidded.

Talia kept working, lining a wooden soap box with paper-thin shevia bark, and mixing the rest of the ingredients. To the oils and lye she added honey and salt, and gave it a good stir. After dividing the mixture into two smaller buckets, she added fine charcoal powder to one, and rich pink mud to the other. They'd be perfect bars—colorful, bubbly, and useful.

The worst part of this would be the mixing. All. By. Hand. She set to work. Careful not to slosh the lye, Talia stirred and stirred. She and her mother talked about her parents' hatanii. Her anticipation became unbearable the more they talked. She'd heard all the stories before, but this was *her* turn, *her* story. And her mother's sweet voice was almost taunting, because she and Talia's father *knew* who her betrothed was. They may have never met the man in person, but they'd met with the island elders to discuss her match, as well as the man's parents, and they'd approved. She would not meet him until the first day of hatanii, far from her childhood home.

"You have all of his gifts planned?" her mother asked, continuing to watch.

"Ayo." Talia swatted in her mother's direction. "Leave me alone. You're just playing with me now."

Her mother grinned. "You'll be happy, Tali." Calm assurance filled her words. Talia was excited, but also terrified. He might be the neighbor from down the street, or a stranger from one of the dozen inhabited islands in the kingdom she'd yet to step foot on.

She looked up from her work, hesitating. "You're sure?" Talia eyed her mother's hatanii mark, a magik tattoo on her temple that matched only one other in this kingdom, in this world—one on her soulmate, on her hatanii partner.

Smiling brightly, her mother drew a deep breath. "I'm sure. Keep an open mind. Trust the process. Treasure the experience." She gave Talia a reassuring squeeze on the shoulder. "I'll leave you to work."

Talia hummed as she completed her task, layering the pink mud soap mix over the black charcoal. Once it was spread and decorated as well as she could get it with her spatula, she stepped back and admired it. What a touch of magik wouldn't do for the top design… She'd always loved swirling beautiful patterns with her magik. A manual design would have to do for now. All that was left was to clean up and allow it to cure. Soon enough, their gifts would be exchanged, and then the ceremony would be right around the corner.

While the tasks had to be completed without magik, the rules didn't specify the cleanup had to be. With a flick of the wrist, she floated the dishes and tools into a box to allow the still-caustic soap to safely cure before scraping and washing them clean. She more gently swished her fingers in the air to send the full soap box to a curing shelf in the work shed, and snapped her fingers to clean up any spilled ingredients on the workbench.

Wearing a contented smile, she rinsed her hands in a basin of fresh, cool water. Hatanii might not take a full month if they could use more magik to build their homes. But even as she thought it, her cheeks warmed. Hatanii was a month of seclusion. She was well aware it was not just about building a physical home together. It was about *fully* exploring their new relationship.

Chapter Two

A dozen couples would be in this hatanii group, matched from various islands in the kingdom, and relocated to a new home. Stepping into adulthood, it was time they left behind the things of their childhood.

On the first morning of hatanii, Talia stood on the assigned dock, her nerves and excitement nearly overflowing. Her cream sarong was tied up perfectly, and she'd made sure to wear a matching pair of shorts underneath to forestall any rubbing. The discomfort of chafed thighs was the last thing she wanted on the day she was to meet her life partner.

Three other hatanii brides from her island joined her on the dock with their families. The participating grooms would be meeting on a different dock at a later time.

Talia's father kissed her on the forehead and wished her well. Her mother straightened the plumeria in her hair, kissing her on both cheeks. "Be happy, Tali." Her smile was bright.

"I'll miss you two," Talia said. And she would. She loved her family, and this village, this island. But even though she was moving away and would be starting a family of her own, she would visit often. And likely right after the month of hatanii—most of her belongings were still here.

Talia's father handed her large woven bag of necessities over to the captain of the ferry, and soon enough, all the hatanii brides were on their way.

It was a tepid day on calm waters, and the girls didn't chat much right away, likely all too excited or nervous. Talia anxiously rubbed the silver charm she'd been gifted by her hatanii partner. It had arrived in her box of gifts a week ago, and since the giver must remain secret until the reveal during hatanii, she'd worn it with the charm hidden on a longer chain underneath her top. Now, she could wear it openly and proudly. It rested a couple of inches below the base of her neck on a medium-length chain.

"Is that from your parents?" a girl asked. "Or *him?*"

Talia bit her lip, her cheeks warming. "Him."

The other brides showed off their gifted jewelry. One wore a carved wooden hair comb, another a pearl bracelet, and the last an impressive coronet decorated with shells. They were all elegant, but Talia liked hers best. It was simple and small, delicate and intricately cast.

Upon reaching their new island, the brides were greeted by kingdom elders and young assistants who divided the brides. The women exchanged hugs and followed as instructed. An unused section of this foreign island would become their new home for the next month, and likely for life.

Talia's heart nearly beat out of her chest when she spotted the framework that was to be her home, the land that was to be hers, *theirs.* It had been purchased and prepared by both her parents and the parents of her groom. Her parents had been gone for a few days with his, building the foundation of the home, the central beams, the outdoor shower and toilet room.

In the center of the flooring lay a single bed. Warmth rose in her cheeks again. She doubted she'd cozy up that quickly to her groom, no matter how perfect the hatanii match was supposed to be. They would take their time, and if he was indeed her perfect match, he would be content to wait.

The young assistant set Talia's woven bag next to the bed and bowed. "Welcome to your hatanii." His boyish smile was sweet. The elder briefly showed her around the property and pointed in the direction where their daily meals could be collected from. There was already a stash of food for the first day and night of the ceremony—fresh mangos, coconuts, crackers, nuts, and more. One of the few magik-powered items was a cooler to keep goat cheese and celebratory juice chilled.

The foundation of the home was on stilts for high tides and unfavorable weather, the surrounding area consisting of sand and wild grasses, with banana trees on the perimeter.

The only other piece of furniture on the foundation was a sturdy table. And on it sat a box.

Eventually, a bell rang in the distance, and Talia's stomach flipped. *He's here. He's* actually *here!*

"Please step to this side of the table for me, Talia," the elder instructed.

She did as ordered, facing away from the table, trying not to fidget with her sarong, the flower in her hair. She *did* straighten her charm on its chain, though. She sucked in her gut, but then loosed it with a breath. He would be seeing all of her curves, accepting her as she was.

Featherlight footsteps rustled through the sand, and then padded on the steps and bamboo flooring, growing closer. She wrung her hands in anticipation.

The table behind her screeched in movement.

"Avanna, you're supposed to *guide* him," an older voice lightly chastised.

"Sorry," a young girl said.

"It's alright," a new voice said, deep and soft, letting out a small chuckle.

Talia's heart melted on the spot.

"Facing away, and then the blindfold, Avanna," the elder instructed.

"You're too tall," the girl whispered loudly.

"Then allow me to lower my head." His voice had a warm familiarity, but it wasn't one Talia actually recognized, though she hadn't made a practice of meandering her childhood island with her eyes closed to discern voices.

A few heartbeats later, the two elders thanked the young girl and boy—the assistants—for their help, and dismissed them from the property.

All Talia had to do was listen, and then turn to see the man she'd spend the rest of her life with. She could barely breathe, her anticipation rising.

The two elders weren't exceptionally long-winded, but they gave speeches about the importance of hatanii, the symbolism of building a life together, and a recap of the process to find their match, to bring them together this day.

The weather wasn't overly warm, but Talia started to sweat in ungracious ways, taking slow breaths.

"It is time. Turn and meet your partner."

Trying to keep an attractive but natural smile on her face, Talia turned, as did her groom.

And her smile vanished instantly. Her stomach on the floor, she gaped.

Carner Davaio stood before her. *Carner Davaio.* The *last* man she'd expected, and the *last* man she'd ever agree to spend her life with.

He'd grown tall and strong since they'd ended their childhood friendship, since his father had taken a position as a lower chief on a larger island, and they'd moved away. But it was *definitely* Carner. His black hair was wavy, his complexion slightly darker than her own. He wore a groom's sarong, and the puka necklace she'd made as one of her gifts. His shock also registered, his eyes wide. "Tali—"

"No," she gritted out, facing the elders. "No." She pointed at Carner. "This is a mistake. He is *not* my hatanii."

The elders looked surprised. "There is no mistake, Talia Mehaven. Carner Davaio is your match."

Then I was never meant to wed. She would never wed someone weak, rude, and insufferably arrogant. "My parents approved of this?!"

"Of course they did."

"Ayo." She rubbed her forehead. "This is a mistake. I wish to contest."

"Do you … also … wish to contest, Carner?"

A moment of silence. "Yes. I contest."

Good. He ought to. And of course he would. She didn't even want to look at him again.

"Do you have grounds you wish to cite?" an elder asked Talia.

She wasn't about to share that. Carner knew what he'd done, and that was enough. "That's private."

The elder lifted an eyebrow at Carner, but he gave no vocal response.

"Then … this hatanii is contested."

Talia stared down at her hands, devastated. You only got one chance at hatanii. One. The interviews, the magik testing, everything… And she had been matched with *him*?

"What… What exactly does this entail?" Carner asked softly, cautiously.

"To be released from the match, the original timeframe and building tasks remain intact."

What?! That was a waste now. This home would be built for no one.

"The full month?" Carner asked.

"Yes. And the full home. It gives you an opportunity to reconsider. Not all matched couples immediately take to one another." The elder tilted her head slightly. "If you complete the tasks and both still contest at the end of the month, then you will be released."

Talia wouldn't be reconsidering, despite the gutting consequences. She would become an akaii—an unwed, the lonely, an old maid. She'd be all but an outcast.

But she would not settle. Her parents had taught her to never settle. Hatanii was about dreams and hope for the future, about love and equality. Carner was none of those things to her.

"As long as we complete the month and build the house, and don't…" She swallowed, utterly embarrassed. *Consummate.* "Don't do anything that involves the marks, then we're free?"

"Yes. One additional task is required. When all but one of the days has passed, we will ring the bell and provide that task."

Talia hugged herself, suddenly more self-conscious of her body, of the fact she'd still have to suffer through an entire month with Carner. "Okay. We'll see you then."

The elders only nodded, disappointment painting their faces. "We continue to wish you blessings for your ceremony. The tasks and tools are in the box on the table. Enjoy your month."

Enjoy? No, there would be no joy. Not for the next month, not for the rest of Talia's life. Her dreams had been built so big, and were now washing away with the riptide that was this botched ceremony.

Chapter Three

An hour later, Talia sat on the sand at a nearby cove. A map had been included in their box of instructions and tools. This cove was near two other hatanii couples' properties. Her face was still warm with anger. *Those* couples were likely happy, getting acquainted with their new loves.

This is ridiculous.

"You do look beautiful today, Tali." Carner's voice came from behind her. "I'm sorry it wasn't for the groom you'd hoped for."

She just shook her head.

"You … don't think you look beautiful?" His tone held hesitation.

Talia threw a glare over her shoulder. She didn't need his approval or anyone else's. And he was the *last* person she cared to have comment on her body.

"Well… I cut up some mango at our… At the house… If you'd like some…"

"No thank you," she muttered.

Silence. "Okay."

Sand rustled behind her, and she shook her head again. *Why Carner? Of all the men out there, why Carner?*

They had been best friends as young children. They'd laughed and giggled and played until dark. Their mothers were best friends—

hatanii brides at the same matching ceremony. And then right around the time other girls in their village had developed their chests, Talia didn't. She eventually did, though it now was only as large as her midsection, depending on her posture. She wasn't as self-conscious about her body now as she used to be. Plenty of women on her island had wide arms, thick legs, and stomach rolls like she did.

But her chest… As a young girl, she hadn't thought much about the changes in their bodies, until one particular day—the day their friendship had ended. The day *he* had ended it.

Talia had been up in her favorite climbing tree while Carner and a few neighborhood boys wandered the dirt lane. One of the boys had said her name, and then playfully pushed Carner.

"Tali? Gross! Never," Carner had said. And then he'd grabbed his own chest, making a gesture about there being nothing there, and laughed, the others crowing after him.

She would never forget his betrayal. He'd stuck up for her before, but now he was mocking her for something she had no control over. She would never forget the way he made her feel that day, and how much she had cried.

And when she'd stopped by his family home the next day, he'd acted happy to see her. She'd punched him in the nose and stalked back to her own home.

It wasn't much later that his father had been elected as a lower chief, and they'd moved away. She'd been glad for it.

As they were still friends, Talia's mother liked to pay Carner's mother a visit whenever they had cause to ferry to the larger island Carner's family now lived on. Talia often had to go with her, and she'd dreaded each visit. Carner was usually lurking in a corner somewhere, and when they'd catch each other's gaze, he'd give the most arrogant smirk.

Luckily, she hadn't been required to visit his home for about two years now. She would have been happy never seeing him again.

Talia closed her eyes, leaning back and propping herself up on her elbows. Hatanii was supposed to be flawless. But now she felt empty, betrayed all over again. She glanced at the charm on her chain as it lay on her chest. The necklace he'd made for *her*. More like for the bride he'd *thought* he would be happy with. She grasped the thin chain, yanking it off, and studied the charm. He had engraved tiny bird-of-paradise flowers into the silver. And now she hated everything about it. She chucked it as far as she could throw, and to her disappointment, it landed on a sandbar. She huffed.

The wards on their property prohibited magik on most aspects of the build, but not on personal things. The cove was technically shared property anyway. She ought to have used her magik to pelt the necklace into the depths of the ocean before her.

Breathing deeply, she rested there for another hour or more, pondering her life, taking in the soothing waves and distant call of gulls.

***

She had to eat eventually, and her stomach was already protesting the lack of food, as she'd only had a small meal that morning. Talia ambled back to the property.

Carner lay on the bed mere feet from the table, his legs crossed as he stared into the sky. He said nothing.

Fruit and cheese had been sliced, laid on the table with crackers. She took a banana leaf and scooped some up for herself. She hesitated as she took some of the mango. Carner continued to stare up at the sky. He'd cut extra for her, an act of civility. And they ought to be civil if they were going to have to endure each other's presence for an entire month. "Thank you," she said softly.

Carner pursed his lips for a long moment. "You're welcome."

She filled a cup with fresh water.

"Do you want to get started on the house after eating?" he asked.

"No. We have an entire month to complete it." They certainly wouldn't be wasting extra time in that bed doing *other things* like the other couples.

"A month isn't all that long when it's done mostly without magik, Tali. And when neither of us are professional builders."

She clenched her teeth. "Talia, Carner. It's Tali-*a*."

He rolled over on the bed, looking at her with brows knit. "Don't your parents still call you Tali?"

That was immaterial. "My family can. My friends can. But you? You can call me by my given name."

His face unreadable, he stared at her for a long while, then averted his gaze. She took her food and drink, and marched back to the cove for peace.

***

By the time Talia returned from the cove, sunset painted the sky. Carner still lay on the single, solitary little bed. It wasn't actually *that* little, but it certainly seemed a lot smaller now… *Why didn't we think to ask for a second bed before the elders deserted us?* They had no way to contact them in seclusion. Though she wasn't even sure if they would have granted the request.

Talia made a simple gesture over her head to light the lamps on the property.

They dimmed.

She gestured again to get them brighter.

"They don't need to be that bright, Tali-*a*," Carner said, stressing the *A*, as the lamps once again dimmed by his hand.

She rolled her eyes. She'd forgotten they were equally matched in lighting magik, so this might have to be a compromise. Stepping up onto the bamboo flooring, Talia crossed her arms and looked down at Carner. "Are we going to take turns on the bed, then?"

He stretched. "I don't see why we have to take turns being miserable. This is large enough for two. We napped next to each other on sleeping mats when we were young…"

"That was… This is…" Talia blinked. "This is a bed meant for … *wed* couples. It's hardly a sleeping mat for young children." It didn't help his case that he was only wearing that sarong, his entire upper body exposed.

They just stared at each other.

Finally, she rested her hands on her hips. "It would be civil to take turns."

Carner gave her that wicked grin. "Civil? Like how you respected the elders today? Or me? *You* contested this hatanii. *You* can take a turn on the ground and let me know how that goes."

"You contested, too."

"You contested first."

She clenched her jaw. "We'll share. Don't touch me."

His expression leveled out. "Wouldn't even if you wanted me to."

After using the shower and toilet on the edge of the property, she returned in her shorts and a sleeveless shirt. He had taken off his sarong to reveal shorts underneath. *Great, even less clothed.* Admittedly, he wasn't ugly. He had more of a gut than her father, and a flattering nose and ears, but looks were only a small part of what made up a person. Her heart ached at that. He hadn't understood that when they were younger, and she doubted he would have changed.

He took a turn at the toilet as she climbed into bed and clung to the edge on the side he hadn't been lying on. When he returned, he slipped under the covers and extinguished the lamps.

After a few minutes of tossing and turning, he huffed.

"What?" she asked.

"Just … can't sleep."

And what was she supposed to do about that? She was sticking to her side and trying to *quietly* fall asleep.

"How is your father?" he asked. "I haven't seen him in ages."

"He's well."

"Still fishing?"

That was a stupid question. He'd been a fisherman his entire life. "Yes… My family does still need food and money…"

"I always liked him. He told the best stories growing up."

She frowned, memories flooding her of the pair of them giggling and listening to her father share the wildest tales from his time on the ocean. She wasn't sure half of them were even true.

"And your mother is still well?" Carner asked.

"Yes."

"Hmm." He paused. "I forgot she made soap. Always brings my mother a bar of her favorite kind when she comes to visit." Nostalgia sweetened his voice. "I guess I should have had a clue that it could be you, with the gift…"

Talia swallowed. *Please don't bring up the gifts. Not the ceremony. Not this disappointment and disaster and heartbreak.*

"I made sure to bring some for us to use," he said.

She sighed loudly. "Maybe if I don't wash myself while we're here, you'll forfeit the bed."

He chuckled. "It's very good soap."

"Can we stop talking about the soap?"

The bed shifted behind her, and in an all-too-close-and-intimate whisper, he added, "A man wonders what kind of bride sends a gift she made with her hands that was meant to touch *every inch of his body*…"

Her eyes shot open. She had not intended it that way *at all*. "It's *hand* soap."

"Hmm… It looks like the bars your mother brings to mine, and we've always used them in the shower…"

And at that last taunt, Talia balled her fists and used her magik to shove him off the bed without laying a single finger on him.

He landed with a firm thud, groaning. She didn't even feel bad about it. He was a strong healer, having obtained that skill from both of his parents. He'd survive. "Thanks for volunteering to take the floor," she gloated.

A rustle broke the momentary silence, and he yanked the blanket right off her. "Wed or not, I believe in compromise. Enjoy the bed tonight."

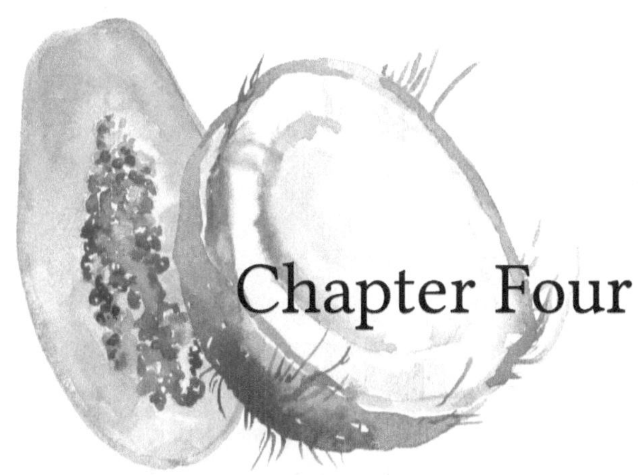

Chapter Four

Did Talia wake up multiple times shivering? Yes. Was it worth it to have the entire bed to herself to sprawl out on? Also yes. Though … waking multiple times hadn't done much for restful sleep.

She woke to a knife chopping nearby, and squinted at the sunshine. She moaned. *Why couldn't it have been a bad dream?* At least a knife had been provided for their use, so she wouldn't have to pull out the one in her bag for meals—the one Carner had hand-carved the handle of as one of her betrothal gifts.

"You look *lovely* in the morning," Carner crooned.

"Go away." She put her pillow over her head.

"We need to get going for breakfast soon. What little food we have left will not be enough to get us through the day."

Removing the pillow from her face, she considered. "I'll skip breakfast. We'll take turns getting supplies."

"Couples get supplies together. Do you want the others talking?"

Ugh. She didn't. The one exclusion to their seclusion—breakfasts with the other couples, those who were supposed to become their closest village friends. Every morning of the ceremony, they were to meet in a central location where fresh food and supplies were flashed in. Flashing was a rare and strong gift, and it was a shame Talia hadn't been born with it: she'd flash in their food *and* another bed.

"Fine." She sat up in bed, her hair a tangled mess. He already had his sarong back on.

"You make beautiful sand art," he said, dropping some pineapple chunks into a banana leaf.

She furrowed her brow for a moment before she remembered. She'd used her magik back at the cove, gently pushing the sand in pretty designs for hours. "Oh. Thanks."

He sat on the edge of the flooring, dangling his feet over the edge and popping pineapple into his mouth. "I imagine you could make beautiful designs in…"

It was almost like they'd had the same thought at the same moment. Beautiful designs in *her* home someday. In *their* home. In *this* home. And she'd hoped to; she'd practiced a special kind of wood burning with her design work. It would have been lovely, complementing the home decoration he'd crafted for her as his third betrothal gift. She would've had to wait to do it until after the magik wards of hatanii had been lifted from the property, but she would have loved to do it.

Carner cleared his throat. "You plan to move back in with your parents?"

As she nodded, her heart broke that much more. She was supposed to build a life with a partner, with a soulmate. "I'll never forgive them for this."

He finished eating his pineapple and stood. "Keep talking like that, Tali…" His voice was soft, almost even hurt. "And I'll manage to forget we were *ever* friends." He eyed her, his expression indiscernible. "Get dressed."

She pulled a new sarong from her packed bag, considering what he'd just said. He was mad at her? Why? He'd contested the arrangement as well. She was too flat-chested, too loud, too … whatever at this point. His shock and disappointment had been on display for all to see at the reveal.

As soon as she announced she was ready, they stomped off, the second breakfast bell chiming in the distance. Halfway there, the path didn't look quite right.

"You're sure it's this way?" she asked.

"Yes."

"Because those trees—"

"It's the right path," he said, curt. "They showed the grooms the location before the reveals."

"Fine. You don't have to get angry."

"Have I got us lost before?"

She plodded along, her sandals sinking into the loose sand. "Yes. That one time when we were exploring the bay. When we came home well past dark, and I wasn't allowed to spend time away from the house for a week as punishment."

Carner huffed. "Fine. One time. And I still got us back safely." He stopped abruptly, facing her. "And I was a *little boy*. You might not have noticed, but I'm a grown man now. And it is daylight. And I'm capable of simple navigation." His nostrils flared. "Maybe you could trust me?"

A challenge. Trust him? With her heart, her emotional well-being? No. With getting them to breakfast? Perhaps. She gestured at the path. "Lead on."

By the time they arrived, all eleven of the other couples had already grabbed breakfast and were sitting on long benches. All the women at one, the men at the other. Not a requirement, but no doubt done for gossiping.

Talia scooped up her breakfast and sat at the last open seat with the other brides. "Almost got lost."

One hummed, licking her fingers. "We'd all bet you'd have your ceremonial marks with how late you two were."

That was mortifying. The marks only appeared once things had been fully consummated between a couple. "Definitely not on the first night…" She cringed.

"Not too loud," one bride warned playfully. "Serena might hear you."

Who's Serena? Talia scanned the table, and then her eyes grew wide as one of the brides leaned forward to talk with those opposite her. On her temple, permanent black swirls and dots had appeared, fresh and bright. *"The first night?!"* Talia whispered.

A couple of the brides around her giggled. "They've been seeing each other for two years."

Talia slumped in her seat. That was unfair. Most youth chose not to date because they didn't want to form too close of an attachment to someone just to discover they weren't their match through hatanii. This bride had enjoyed the last two years and then, out of every eligible groom in the kingdom, had been matched with the one she already loved. And Talia was stuck with…

She glanced over her shoulder at the men as they chatted away about their own matters. Her stomach churned. Carner was surrounded by them, like he'd been surrounded by young boys on the lane when he'd mocked her.

"So, tell us about your partner, Talia," one of the girls prompted.

Talia faced her, digging into her food. "Well, uh…" She didn't need any judgment, or to have to keep track of lies. "I actually know mine from when we were little."

"Really?" the woman asked excitedly. "Sounds like we know who'll show up with their mark soon." A couple more brides giggled.

Talia groaned internally. Not soon, not on the last morning of hatanii, not ever.

"Which one is he?"

She looked over her shoulder again. "Second from the left, facing us." And in that moment, Carner's gaze met hers. He cracked a crooked smile and winked. The brides giggled again, and Talia tried to hide a scowl. He liked to play games just to torture her. This was going to be a long month.

Still smiling, Carner leaned toward the man next to him and pointed directly at Talia, whispering something. The others started to turn, and Talia could have died of embarrassment right on the spot. She whipped around in her seat, staring at her plate.

The women teased her about the men's eyes on her. "Definitely going to be the next one with a mark."

If only the earth would swallow her whole. She wasn't ready to become an akaii already. She and Carner had agreed that no one had to know yet that they'd contested the arrangement. It would be a long and awkward month. "We've agreed to take things slow."

The rest of breakfast was uncomfortable, but at least the chatter shifted between the brides, most of whom she'd yet to meet. They introduced themselves and talked about their betrothed; some had started to build their homes.

Couples started leaving the breakfast tables together to go back to their properties. Talia was tense. She was tired of the gossip, but she also didn't want to go back to seclusion with Carner. A light brush on her shoulder startled her, and she looked up. Carner wore a softer smile this time. "Shall we go?"

"Yeah." They approached the supply tables where their lunch and dinner for the day had been preportioned.

Hefting bags of food and drink, they trekked back toward the property. "Why do you do that?" she asked when she was sure they were out of earshot.

"Do what?"

"Wink. And smile. And constantly mock me," she clarified.

"You wanted everyone to think we weren't contesting."

She rolled her eyes. "You don't have to be *that* convincing." Her heart hurt at the old memory. "And you don't have to gossip about me with your new friends."

"I ... didn't gossip." His tone conveyed confusion. "Why do you think I was gossiping?"

"Ayo." As if laying on the flirtatiousness and then whispering to friends wasn't something he had a record of doing...

"I didn't gossip. They wanted to know which of the beautiful women I was winking at."

"Then stop winking at me. And stop bringing up soap in bed."

"You're inviting me back to bed?"

She adjusted the pineapple poking her from a bag. "No. I'm just saying ... leave me alone, and we can endure this in peace."

He grabbed her arm. "Tali."

"What?!" She raised her voice.

He shifted the bag under his arm. "We may not leave here wed, but we *could* be friends again."

She studied him, his dark brown eyes those of a little boy she'd once have chosen to go on any adventure with. "I didn't sign up for hatanii to make friends."

He pressed his lips into a thin line. "You don't think partners should be friends as well as lovers? If you had been matched with a stranger, wouldn't you want to also consider him a friend?"

She didn't have an answer to that. Of course partners should be lovers *and* friends. But she genuinely didn't know what to say. "I expected it all." Her mother's words haunted her. *Trust the process. Treasure the experience. You'll be happy, Tali.* All lies. "I suppose it's all or none." She turned and kept walking back to their assigned property.

***

It was silent and cold between them when they emptied their arms of the day's food. She didn't much care to build a home she would never inhabit, but if they worked away at it, at least it gave her something to do while they spent endless hours and days together.

Only speaking minimally, they delved into the provided tools and piles of bamboo and lumber. Instructions had been included. Work was slow and painstaking. Neither was a builder by trade, but they had the basics down. It would go *so* much faster with magik.

At least the weather was cool. As they took a much-needed dinner break, Talia rested against a boulder, viewing their work.

Carner followed suit, sitting close to her. "Not bad. I bet we've made more progress than most."

She shoveled down a handful of steamed cassava. "Probably."

"And your work is really nice."

She furrowed her brow, eating another handful. What kind of backhanded compliment was that? "You thought I'd come unprepared? That I wouldn't put in equal work or equal quality to you?"

"No… I just thought you might want to cut corners since you don't want to keep this as a home…"

She hid a frown. This had been a dream for her. A quiet new community, friends, a home of her own as a woman. A partner for life. Love. "Just because I won't live here doesn't mean whoever ends up moving in doesn't deserve a quality home. I have work ethic."

Carner stretched out his legs in front of him. "Are you always this pleasant? You used to be funny and nice and sweet. You've been a viper since before I moved away."

The absolute audacity… "Me? A viper?" She twisted her head to face him. "*You've* been an arrogant, two-faced boar since before you moved away."

He scoffed. "How so?"

"First of all, your stupid, condescending sneer. The one you like to taunt me with."

He swatted a hand dismissively. "I don't sneer."

"Yes, you do." She took a sip of water.

"Like how?"

She tried to replicate his stupid crooked grin.

"I don't look like that."

"Yes, you do."

"If I looked like *that*…" He pointed at her. "Then people would laugh in my face, because that's comical."

She rolled her eyes. "It's the motive behind that look you give me. Here on this island, and anytime I've been to your family's new island to visit. Always sneering, never apologetic. You're not the boy I once knew and liked."

His reply bordered on condescension. "No, I'm not. I've grown up. So have you, but maybe not in all ways."

She took another bite of food, shaking her head in frustration.

"I *don't* give you condescending looks, Tali. I'm sorry if you don't like the way I smile. That's just … part of me. I've smiled like this for as long as I can remember. I can't change that."

"Right." Something he couldn't change. Just like she couldn't have changed how quickly her chest grew in as a girl, but that hadn't stopped him from mocking her. "Two-faced."

"When have I ever been two-faced?"

She choked down the rest of her food. "The fact that you have chosen to forget is evidence that it does not matter to you. That my feelings and our friendship *never* mattered." Her ears were burning.

"Then remind me. What did I do?"

Talia clenched her jaw. "What happened before I punched you in the face?"

"You mean before you went crazy and broke my nose for no reason?"

She stared at him, waiting for him to recall what he'd done the day before she'd hit him, the things he'd said.

"I don't know why you hate me," he repeated.

Sighing, she stood and brushed the sand from her backside. "Let it be something you think about as we continue to fulfill our tasks."

They labored in silence on the home until sunset. They'd both worked up a healthy sweat during the day.

"Do you mind if I shower first?" he asked.

"Fine."

Minutes later, he emerged from the shower, again in shorts. She caught herself cracking the tiniest of smiles at his hair. She'd forgotten how curly it got when wet.

He threw his thumb over his shoulder. "My bar of soap is on the left. I put a separate one out for you on the right, so you don't have to share."

"Thank you." It had been thoughtful, but it didn't fix things.

As she turned the soap in her hands in the shower, she allowed herself to cry. *Trust the process. Treasure the experience. You'll be so happy,*

Tali. This soap had been made for another man. Hatanii had failed her.

After toweling off and dressing, she quickly discovered why he'd claimed the shower first. This way he could take the bed. He lay still as she approached. "I am not giving up the bed tonight," he said. "You can choose the floor or the other side. I don't care. But I am sore and tired."

She considered being stubborn enough to yank the bedding away just as he'd done the night before, and sleeping in the sand, but her hair was still damp, and it really *didn't* sound comfortable. Her muscles groaned as much as his did. "Fine. We'll share. Don't touch me."

Chapter Five

A storm rolled in that night. The wards over the property protected against the rain. The soft pitter-patter of raindrops against an invisible shield overhead was heavenly to fall asleep to. The wards, however, didn't do the best job of keeping out wind and chill. To her utter horror, she woke with her arm around Carner the next morning, no doubt having been cold.

She pulled her arm back very, *very* carefully and would take that secret to her grave.

They walked to breakfast early. The gossip and reports only continued at the segregated tables. To Talia's shock, a second couple arrived with fresh matching bond marks on their temples. This couple had known each other for only two days. Beaming, the girl explained how they'd been perfectly matched, and that they were trusting the elders, trusting the magik and their fate.

The table was crowded, but Talia's heart was lonely. One by one, each couple would follow suit, and more eyes would turn on her to ask how she and Carner were doing. She answered questions about how the house-building was going, and tried to avoid questions about Carner at all costs.

Day in and day out, they worked together relatively well. The house blueprints were already drawn out for them, but they still communicated on places where they had to make decisions. They took turns preparing food, and asked each other for help with holding or hammering things when needed. After a while, the frigid silence turned to reflective calm. No scowls, no arrogant smirks. She could get through this.

The hardest part was considering her future once this was done. Yes, she wanted to be done with this task. She wanted to be free from the arrangement she and her parents had made, but she was terrified of her future. To be an akaii, an outcast, was not something people undertook lightly. They were defying tradition, defying the elders. She'd never personally met an akaii, but whispers followed those who were, for the rest of their lives. They almost certainly never found love, formed their own families, or experienced what it was like to step out on their own. They were usually a burden to their families.

But every time Talia reconsidered her situation, two things came to mind. The way Carner had made her feel as a girl, and the way he had also contested this from the beginning.

After a dream about becoming a homeless old hag one night, she woke to Carner's arm around her. He was touching her, like she'd told him not to. But part of her imagined it was her true soulmate's arm, that his warmth could take away her pain, as opposed to him being the cause of it. She stared at a nearly finished wall and lay there, wishing.

The warmth of his arm lingered with her through the day. It was just the loneliness. Hatanii was probably all a lie. There were no blessings, no perfect matches. It was about squashing the defiant into utter loneliness until they settled. But then again, if she accepted all the negative things she thought about how unlucky she'd been to be paired with Carner, she had to ask if that meant the same about herself. If he was equally unlucky. There was nothing so wrong with Talia. It was just the fates having a laugh at both their expense.

But the fact remained: she was lonely. At dinner that day, they sat near each other, admiring the progress they'd made. Two of the four walls lined with bamboo now stood securely attached to the flooring.

Carner pointed to the top of the building. "I bet we could do the roof in a week."

She savored a slice of mango. "Maybe."

He gave her a smile, one that quickly mellowed. "You're a good partner, Tali. I mean, Talia. And ... *building* partner..."

She picked through some nuts. "You too." Perhaps they could at least come out of this as friends. Or acquaintances again? "How are your parents?"

"Oh, well. Father's always busy. Mother's happy enough. Siblings are well."

"Mmm." She didn't hear from her older siblings as often as she'd like. "My siblings are well, too."

His smile brightened. "Remember when Calypso tried to capture a monkey to bring it home as a pet?"

Talia laughed. "Yes." His older sister had pulled some pretty crazy antics growing up.

"Well, she finally caught one, and she keeps it in her home now."

Talia giggled. "No she didn't."

"Yes, she did." He was adamant, a hand to his heart, that soft boyish face now more intense with maturity.

"You're making that up, Carner. You were always a bad liar!"

His lip twitched. "You don't have to believe me, but it's true."

She arched an eyebrow. His insistence made her pause. "Truly?"

And then out slid that wicked grin.

She chucked a nut at him, and he laughed.

"Ayo... I knew it!"

He bent over from laughing so hard.

"You're not funny!" Shaking her head, she smiled. They'd shared plenty of fun adventures as children. She wished they *had* stayed friends. That he hadn't changed.

Eventually, Carner calmed his laughing, studying Talia. "I miss this." He paused. "Your laugh. Your smile."

At that, her smile faded.

"Why do you do that?" he asked gently.

"Please don't," she whispered. "Just don't." Voicing her pain would make her weak, would give him ammunition. She wrung her hands. "I… I wouldn't mind if we made our way back to being friends."

There was longing in his eyes. "I would love to be your friend again."

***

The second week of hatanii, they continued to work hard on the home, and on slowly rebuilding their friendship. They reminisced about their childhoods, and shared stories about what had happened to them after Carner had moved away. But things got awkward and silent when any discussion of the future came up.

She'd had dreams for the future, and about what she could contribute to a partnership. It was important to be well-rounded in their society because most people chose to be matched, and doing so meant accepting that there was a strong likelihood you would be uprooted. A variety of skills would be necessary to help you find your bearings in a new village, discovering where you could specialize to fit the local needs in support of your household and community.

Talia favored the arts—soapmaking, design work—though she was warming up to more physically demanding tasks as they built this house. Her arms and legs were already stronger from all the physical labor.

As a wed woman, she would have choices. As an akaii, she would have to take anything she could get.

Carner discussed some of his skills and education, what career paths he'd considered taking. He wasn't interested in being a chief like his father. He mentioned how much he'd enjoyed mentoring local children on his parents' island. The very image of that softened Talia's heart a degree. He was kind … most of the time. He too would become an akaii once this month ended, once the match had officially been dissolved by the elders.

Talia tried not to dwell on either of their futures beyond the next couple of weeks.

It was lovely getting to know the other brides and grooms each morning at breakfast. That extra time balanced out the quiet, balanced out the awkwardness between Talia and Carner. Except for the pain it brought each time a new couple showed up with matching marks— a reminder that they'd made a lifelong commitment of love. Her feet were always a little heavier leaving breakfast after watching the other couples pair off and head away to their sanctuaries.

She and Carner made great progress on the home, and would likely finish it well before the deadline. But they didn't slow down. Work filled the time, the occasional silence.

During the third week of the build, the shevia bark roof came together quickly, partially thanks to magik. The wards allowed specific magik to be used in the construction process, as the instructions given to them laid out.

Carner was high up on a ladder, securing a beam. Talia had returned to the floor to take a short water break. She eased herself onto the bamboo floor, crossing her ankles and leaning back against the wall. As she did so, a sharp prick in her back made her jump.

"Ack!"

"What's wrong?" Carner looked down at her.

"Ouch!" It burned. "I'm not sure. I think… I think a bee."

Without hesitation, Carner descended the ladder and set down his tools. "Where?"

She cringed. "My upper back."

He crouched, and she leaned forward. His fingers grazed her skin, pushing the fabric of her orange sarong to the side slightly. "The stinger's still in. Hold still." He flicked it out.

She released a breath. "Thanks."

"I can heal that."

Still in pain, she nodded her consent.

His hand slid onto her back, and she sat stiff, not sure how she felt about that. The pain slowly subsided, and he leaned back, smiling.

"As good as I can do." Healing magik had limits. It was most useful for cuts, scrapes, and bruises, but it took the edge off the bee's venom.

She leaned against the wall again, and averted her gaze, staring at an injury on her hand. "Thank you. It's not fair your parents have healing magik and neither of mine do."

"You have skills I don't. We complement each other." He quickly added, "Well, I mean, our places in society, and…"

Perhaps their magik skills assessment played a larger role in the matches than she'd thought. They were equally matched in some magik skills, but they each had abilities the other lacked. "Still…"

"You hurt yourself?" he asked.

She looked up from her sore finger. "Oh, I got a pretty big sliver. I was finally able to dig it out, but it still hurts."

He kneeled, holding out his hands. "May I?"

Two weeks ago, she would have been happy to be riddled with slivers and never accept his help, but agreeing to be friends had eased that tension. "Sure."

He took her hand in his, and his lips quirked upward. As he studied the hand he was healing, she looked him over. He still wore the necklace she'd given him. At times, she'd wanted to rip it from his neck and grind those shells into powder. Why did he still wear it if not to mock her? She wasn't sure she wanted to know the answer, and it was his gift to do with as he pleased.

Carner's touch was soft, awakening something in her stomach she'd rather not have there. A yearning, a desire. With him that close, and still only wearing a sarong around his waist, she didn't hate looking at him, feeling his hands on hers. And her traitorous heart and lungs did her no favors.

It didn't take Carner long to heal her, but his hands lingered. "Any other injuries?"

She swallowed, meeting his eyes. His deep and piercing eyes. "Um, no…"

"Good." He guided her hand to his lips, pressing it to them. "All better."

Her body and heart were traitors. Absolute traitors that tried to make her forget how much she loathed him.

Talia took her hand back, glancing at his chest again. She put her mind in its place, rekindling her annoyances. "Do you own shirts? Or longer sarongs? I trust your father makes enough to afford full clothing."

Carner chuckled. "I don't know about you, but I entered the agreement with expectations of meeting my bride. If I was going to get hot and sticky and sweaty, I imagined it would be doing many things, not only because I was building a home under the summer sun. Wearing more clothing would only make me unnecessarily hotter."

She looked away, her cheeks warming at his bluntness.

"Tell me, Tali," he taunted. "You want me to believe you don't have any outfits hidden in your bag that you haven't worn? That you brought with expectations for nights with your soulmate?"

Her silence spoke her answer.

He was silent a moment too. "Let me know if you injure yourself again. I'm always happy to heal a friend."

Chapter Six

The roof was finished. The walls were finished. They agreed to tackle the windows next—the part of the process that required the most magik. A special jar had been provided for each window—filled with crushed crystal.

This magik was unique to the hatanii process, not something either had done before. Following instructions, they poured the crystal into their hands and stood side by side, uttering the words of a spell, and gently blowing upon the crystals. The crystal shards lifted, swirling in the air, forming a liquid that stretched into the frame of the window and then solidified into clear panels.

Talia and Carner shared toothy smiles at the wonder of it. There was something so poetic about this special magik. There was something almost poetic about their matching callused hands from building this home, too.

With more hesitation, they opened a specific jar they'd saved for last. It was the family window, one that was always built into the east wall so the rising sun could cast the design on the glass into the home. Had they already consummated their relationship, they would have this design etched into their skin. Now, they were about to see it for the first time in the family window.

This jar was different, with a light coating of gold on the clear crystals. The procedure was the same as before. As the crystals swirled in the air, gold streaks formed. It took longer for the magik to do its job on this as it calculated the precise pattern for the mark of their hatanii matching. Once it formed a pane of crystal with a golden pattern embedded, Talia could only stare in wonder. It was breathtaking. It spoke to her soul.

It *ached* in her soul. She stared and mentally traced each line, each dot in this unique pattern. She'd wondered if the magik would somehow not work, but it *had* formed a design. *Their* design, had they chosen to accept their match.

It felt wrong for the magik to still work when they'd contested the arrangement. When they abandoned the ceremony and returned to their respective families' islands, would this house be given to a family in need, and they'd just knock this window out? No one would live in a home bearing another family's mark.

Speechless, Talia kept her eyes fixed on the mark, frowning.

"I'm going for a walk," Carner said, and turned, leaving her alone.

***

Carner didn't come back until dark that night, and wordlessly slipped into bed. Talia had worried about him, but hadn't gone searching. He'd likely been at the cove, doing the same as she was back at the house—sinking into a depression about how the fates had been cruel. How the elders had been cruel.

"Are you okay?" she whispered.

"I'm fine."

They barely spoke the next day. They continued to work on the house, hanging doors and finishing edges.

As they ended the third week, they slowly warmed back up, chatting as old friends. Talia cherished breakfast time now. Not as a way to avoid Carner, but to spend time with new friends. Her heart sank every time she thought about how she was lying to them, about how she was going to have to move back to her parents' home and leave these friends.

It didn't help that all but three of the couples now had hatanii marks. She felt so pressured into the arrangement. Growing up, she'd never imagined she'd resent this ceremony. It was to be a gift, a marvel, a legacy. Now, it was expectations and disappointment.

As they headed into their last week of the ceremony, the house was nearly complete. They'd worked diligently. With only finishing touches to go, they agreed to give themselves some time off.

They spent time at the cove, dipping their feet into the water and talking. They collected rocks and shells and sticks to play games they both knew. One evening they ate dinner together out in the sand, playing one of their games. Carner made a sneaky strategic move and won.

Talia wrinkled her nose, picked up a chunk of pineapple, and chucked it at him, nailing him in the chest.

He gasped, then picked up a piece of roasted fish and hurled it at her, right into her braided hair.

"You did not!"

And then it was a food fight. Minutes later, they were laughing uncontrollably.

"Remember when we threw food in your parents' house?" she asked breathlessly.

He chuckled more. "Yes. I wasn't allowed to go to bed until I cleaned every inch of that room!"

She smiled, surveying herself—sticky with juice, chunks of fish and papaya in her hair. "We really shouldn't have wasted the food."

Carner pulled his arm up to his mouth, licking a spot dripping with juice. "I don't intend to."

"That hungry, huh?"

He shrugged, scraping off a smear of something from his chest with a finger, then licking it. "Still tastes good." He looked up, eyes flirtatious. "Do you want help cleaning up?"

Her stomach flipped. Was he seriously asking if she wanted him to lick and pick food off her? His flirtations were confusing. Had he just become the kind of man who flirted with everyone? Because sometimes it didn't feel like taunting. Sometimes he made her feel … like maybe she *did* want to be more than friends.

But he had *also* contested the arrangement. He had *never* suggested they proceed. He wasn't trying to court her. He was trying to be friends. They'd decided to be friends.

She snapped her fingers to clean off the bulk of the food. "I'm sure I can take care of the rest of it in the shower." And a cold shower it would be, as she tried not to imagine what it would be like for them to share a shower.

***

The next day at breakfast, Talia intentionally sat facing the men's table, occasionally sneaking a peek at Carner.

"So… It's the last week…" one of the brides said.

Talia frowned. "Like I said, we're taking our time."

Carner had grown into a handsome man, that much she could admit. He could be kind when he wanted to be. And he worked hard. Maybe… Maybe it was worth reconsidering the match?

As she was midchew, studying him, he made a gesture to the grooms surrounding him, and they laughed with him. Talia became hollow. The gesture had been a swift swipe down his chest as if to indicate 'flat chest' or 'nothing there.'

She swallowed, assaulted by memories of his mocking. Standing, she took the rest of her food and threw it in the compost bin and stomped away toward their property.

"Talia?" Carner yelled.

She didn't respond.

"Talia! Wait! We need to grab our food for the day."

She kept marching, until a hand wrapped around her arm. "Wait up."

Talia whirled, fist clenched, ripping her arm from Carner's hand. "Touch me again, and you'll remember what it feels like to have me break your nose."

He took two steps back, his brows knit, his jaw slack. "Why are you angry with me?"

"Why?" She repeated his gesture, flat hands to the chest. "That's why."

"What?"

"I can't stand the sight of you, Carner." The fresh sting of his betrayal made her want to take back every fond thought she'd had of him over the last three weeks.

He raised his voice. "I don't even know what you're talking about! I'm tired of this hot and cold, of your riddles! I have no idea what I did to make you break my nose all those years ago, or why you want to do it now!"

Seething, Talia allowed that anger and hurt to build, to simmer. "You don't remember what you did. I will *always* remember. Your words, and how they made me feel. The day before I punched you, I was up in the tree that overhangs the lane. You and your friends were talking about me."

His face still showed confusion.

She made the gesture again. "Flat chest. You said 'Tali? Gross! Never.' And you *laughed* about me. You all did."

A spark of recognition shone in Carner's eyes. "You heard that?"

"It took me forever to get over that. To be confident again. But I *did* get over it. At least I *thought* I had. Until I saw you again, and fate and the elders and our parents thought it was a good idea to shackle me to someone who doesn't respect me, who judges based on appearances, who's arrogant!"

"Tali," he pleaded, taking a step forward.

She gritted her teeth. "It's Talia. And leave me alone." She turned and ran the rest of the way to their property, then past it to the cove. And there she cried.

Less than a week. I just have to make it a few more days, and then I never have to see his face again.

Chapter Seven

A good half hour later, Talia stared at the waves, despondent, no longer crying.

"Ack!" A yelp of pain came from behind her.

She sniffled. "I wouldn't try to cross the line if I were you." She'd drawn a literal line in the sand.

"Ayo! A hex?! Really?" Carner asked.

"I told you to leave me alone."

"For how long?"

"Forever."

"You'll keep the hex active forever? What about food? I returned for our food."

She straightened her back. "I don't need to eat."

"Talia, be reasonable."

She flourished her hand in the air, cutting off all sound. The magik cut off his voice, the crash of the waves, the caw of the gulls, the buzz of the flies and bees. "I'm muffling you, so you are wasting your breath. Go away."

***

Talia sat there for hours, staring at the ocean in utter silence. Twice she looked behind her to find a fresh banana leaf full of food had been left for her. She didn't eat it. She wasn't hungry.

She was angry and hurt, as much at herself as she was at Carner. Her father had always chastised her for having big emotions, for being unforgiving. And it killed her to be that way, to let such a small incident take hold of her so fully, so brutally. But she had fought for the *longest* time to be happy with herself after her best friend's betrayal, and a simple 'I'm sorry' that he might utter wouldn't fix that.

Eventually, she lay down in the sand, lazily drawing designs with her magik. She was tired from the lack of food, from crying, and from using her magik on the designs, the muffling, and the hex. She didn't care.

It wasn't the chill that woke her, but the hard patter of rain on her face. Talia woke with a start, the cove dark, a storm unleashing itself upon the island. She was weak. As hexes were frowned upon, she'd only been trained to use them for self-defense, not for long-term use, and it had drained her. She cried, wallowing in her pathetic state.

A deep grunt came from her right as Carner passed through her weakened hex barrier. He reached for her. "Come to the house, Tali. Please."

She whimpered. "It's not my house."

"I know. Come be warm." He grasped her arms, lifting her slightly. "Let me help you up."

Beyond tired, she forced herself to try to stand, and he aided her, wrapping an arm around her. "Lean on me."

She shuffled her feet toward the property.

"Do you … mind?" he asked. "The hex?"

Extending her foot, she disrupted the line in the sand, and the power fell.

"Thank you." He practically dragged her back, her footsteps heavy, her face screwed into a frown.

"I don't like you," she croaked.

"I know," he said softly. "I wouldn't either if I were you."

With the rain beating down and the wind blowing hard, they were soaked to the bone before they crossed the threshold.

Carner eased her onto a chair they'd made in the bedroom. "You should get changed into something dry."

Newlywed homes only had two rooms, a walled-off bedroom, and the rest of the house—the kitchen and living space where visitors mingled. The shower and toilet remained in a separate room outside, and the house would be expanded as their family grew.

"I can change in the other room," he volunteered. "Do you … need help getting … changed?"

She gave him a look of disgust, though it probably looked more pathetic, like a confused drowned rat. Did she need him to peel her clothes off her? Or rummage through her clothing? No.

"Right… Well, I'll, um… I just don't want you falling over and hurting yourself."

Summoning the rest of her strength, she forced herself to stand. "I'll be fine."

"Okay. Call for me if you need anything." He grabbed shorts and a towel, leaving her alone in the bedroom.

It was a delicate balancing act as she changed, too weak to stand the entire time while she took off the clothes plastered to her. She dressed, leaving her wet clothes on the floor, and then crawled into bed, a disheveled, shivering mess.

After a long while, Carner quietly tapped on the door. "Can I come in?"

"I'm dressed."

He entered, his posture and expression hesitant. "Are you alright?"

"I'm fine."

He studied her a minute. "You're still cold. It took me a while to get past the hex. Do you… I could warm… Or…" He swallowed and sat on the floor, facing her as she lay on her side. "I was not making fun of you at breakfast, Tali. Talia." His voice was gentle, regretful. "I'm sorry you thought so. I was sharing how we had fun yesterday, when we had the food fight." He made the gesture in front of his chest. "Covered in food."

She was beyond stupid. But it didn't change what he'd done all those years ago, and the way it made her feel. And she didn't want to talk about it with a headache pressing in on her.

"Can I get you food?" he asked.

She shook her head.

"You're weak."

"I need sleep."

He eyed her. "Okay. Do you want me to sleep on the floor, or do you want me to … help warm you?"

Her teeth chattering, she hated herself in that moment. She was bitterly cold. Her pride and hurt wanted him to sleep an ocean away, but her body craved warmth. And they still only had the one bed, the one blanket, and he had gotten wet too, trying to help her.

"I won't do anything you don't want," he added cautiously.

"Okay," she whispered, ashamed.

He crawled in behind her, extinguished the lights, and slowly slid a hand along her arm, gently rubbing it. "Is this alright?"

"Yeah."

"I'm so sorry," he whispered. "I never meant to make you feel less than you are. You've always been beautiful to me."

Her heart wrenched. "I just want to sleep."

"Okay."

She woke once during the night, having developed a cough. Carner got her a glass of water and a handkerchief, and soothed her.

In the morning, she still had some residual shivers, was famished, and had a screaming headache and slight cough. There wasn't a whole lot his healing magik could do for it.

Carner frowned, rubbing her arm again. "You don't need to go to breakfast today. I didn't eat much yesterday, so there's still a lot here I can make you, and then I'll go get supplies to last us the rest of the day."

She matched his frown, but accepted. The warm meal he made hit the spot.

After returning from the community breakfast to get food for the rest of the day, Carner relayed everyone's concerns about Talia. It didn't make her feel any better. He'd told them she was a little unwell, though she couldn't help but wonder if some of them had heard her and Carner yelling, or had seen their interactions at the cove.

Eventually, around lunchtime, she forced herself to sit up in bed, her head still pounding, her cough not easing.

Carner sat in the corner of the room, keeping her company. "I completely forgot about what I said and did that day. It was many years ago, and I was young. And stupid."

She picked at her nails.

"I didn't realize you heard or saw that," he said.

Talia shook her head. "Why did you think I busted your nose?"

He let out a wry chuckle. "I had no idea. My brother said girls sometimes start to get a little crazy at that age."

She scowled.

Carner raised his hands. "Which I now realize was horrible."

Sighing, she shook her head again.

"I'll prepare lunch. You rest." He returned a few minutes later with food for them both, taking his position on the floor again. It was nice to have most of the work done on the house so she could recuperate.

Halfway through their meal, Carner spoke again. "I wasn't making fun of you, not really."

"What do you mean?"

He hesitated. "When you were up in that tree. I never made fun of you, not the way you think."

She cocked her head, disbelieving. His words and actions couldn't have been interpreted any other way.

Carner set his meal on the floor beside him, his mouth ajar for some time. "The thing is… We were getting older. Interests change. Our bodies changed." He looked at the floor, all confidence stripped from his expression and voice. "I … started … to like you as more than a friend… But I didn't know what to do with those feelings. And

I was embarrassed to have my friends point it out and tease me. So, I said what came to my mind first. They'd gossiped about other girls having grown…" He gave an awkward shrug. "And you hadn't yet." He looked up, meeting her gaze. "I was never ashamed of you. You were my best friend. I was only ashamed of how I felt. I didn't know what to do with that."

She swallowed a bite of food, not speaking, not sure how to process or respond.

"I was young," he said. "I never would have done that if I had known you would hear or see it. And then I moved away, and you avoided me whenever you came to visit our home."

He had liked her. All those years ago, he had liked her.

"I've always thought you were beautiful and clever." He pursed his lips. "I'm sorry I ruined our friendship."

Chapter Eight

For the next two days, Talia fought off her illness while Carner volunteered to finish the small things in the house that still needed doing. She was on the mend physically, and in her heart. Had it been hurtful the way he'd talked with his friends? Yes. But his reasoning made more sense. They *had* been young.

Two days before the end of the ceremony, Talia lay in bed, having woken from a nap.

Carner entered the bedroom. "The living space is all swept. How are you doing?"

She smiled softly as a lady beetle landed on her hand. "Doing well." She watched as it crawled around, tickling her.

Carner approached and crouched next to her to watch as well. "New friendship."

Had he meant it about theirs? Or about her and the beetle? "I forgive you, Carner."

He gave her a sad smile. "Thank you, Tali." He shook his head. "Sorry, Talia. I might never get used to that. You'll always be Tali to me."

She held her hand out, the beetle strolling down her finger. Carner's smile warmed as he lifted his hand to hers. The beetle took the bridge onto his hand.

"You can call me Tali." She studied Carner's hand. "My friends do." Her heart beat a little faster as their hands remained touching, that familiar and traitorous longing stirring within her. She certainly didn't remember feeling like that when they'd held hands as children.

Carner focused on the beetle. "Maybe… Maybe that's what hatanii was for you. You needed this opportunity to fully heal."

Perhaps? It didn't feel right. Most of the other couples had started with a blank slate, but she and Carner had started with a large deficit. Fate's punishment was to not give them soulmates, but to force them together so he had a chance to apologize, and she had a chance to heal? Perhaps it was fate's way of telling her not everyone was born with a soulmate, and this was the best she could do.

"If we're going to be friends after this… We'll keep in touch?" she asked.

As the beetle flew away, Carner subtly frowned. "We'll see."

She frowned as well. Perhaps even friendship was beyond their grasp at this point. People would wonder why they could be friends, but not wed. Why they had rebelled against the ceremony and elders and even their own families.

Carner narrowed his eyes, looking at their hands. "What happens if only one person contests the match? If only one of us had decided to contest on the first day?"

She studied him, not sure what to make of his question. Had he… "I don't know. I remembered being told contests were allowed, but at the time I didn't care about the details because I didn't expect to need that information…"

Silently, he slid his hand under hers. But he said nothing, still staring at their hands.

He was so unreadable sometimes. And it killed her how much a simple touch from him ached within her. It destroyed her how much his lips almost begged to be kissed. "Do you wish you hadn't contested this?" she dared to ask.

Something flashed across his face. Guilt? Anger? Regret? He rubbed her hand and then retracted his. "I'm going to see if the wash is dry." He stood and walked away, leaving Talia more confused than ever.

That night, Talia struggled to find rest. She weighed her options. She considered her future. Her mind dwelled on her pain and frustration. Carner had joined her wordlessly in bed, but in spirit he was miles away. He breathed softly behind her as she lay on her side. In that moment, she worried about *his* future, *his* desires. Partners or not, friends or not, she wanted him to be happy.

His gentle smiles and genuine apology seeped into her heart. She reflected on all the childhood memories they shared, on all the potential they still had—individually and as a couple. Hatanii was about finding your soulmate, your equal. Had they been so unevenly matched, if she managed to overlook the pain he'd caused? Their magiks complemented each other. So did their education. They could each hold their own in an argument. But something… There was something still lacking, and she couldn't put her finger on it.

Something in her craved being nearer to him. She scooted toward the center of the bed, until her back reached his arm. Carner radiated warmth—his body and his soul. Talia waited for that feeling to disappear, for herself to get annoyed, or for her mind to return to her default anger at the recollection of his childhood betrayal.

It didn't happen.

Carner slowly rolled behind her, an arm sliding onto hers as he snuggled up to her, holding her. Talia's heart beat wildly at his touch, at his bare skin against hers. He was probably only sleeping and hadn't realized what he was doing, only reacting to her movement in bed. But the way his hands had caressed her felt too intentional, too respectful for someone in a deep sleep.

After a few minutes in that position, she worked up the courage to whisper. "What do you want from this, Carner?"

He didn't respond.

***

Talia woke with Carner's arm still draped around her in the morning. She lay there pondering what little time they had left together. Tomorrow was the last day of the hatanii ceremony, an abnormal day. The usual breakfast would occur, but the elders would arrive to congratulate them, and their parents would ferry in shortly after that for a home tour and the evening celebration. At least that was the case for all the happy newlyweds, not akaii who would face the others in shame at their rejection of custom.

The morning before, the tension was thick between Talia and Carner. Neither really spoke as they prepared for breakfast. He'd never answered her question as he held her during the night. It had been a fleeting moment that she'd read too much into, that her heart still yearned to be in.

Unsurprisingly, they were the last of the dozen couples still without their hatanii marks. Everyone greeted Talia kindly, glad she'd recovered from falling ill, but there were questioning glances, concerned looks. She and Carner left earlier than needed. With each footstep back to their property, Talia's heart broke a little more. If he wouldn't say it, maybe she should.

What if? What if they gave it a chance? In the moments they laughed and worked together, she was happy. In the moments he touched her, she either calmed or felt things she hadn't expected to with him.

After arriving at their house, they deposited the day's food on the table. Talia drew a deep breath, bolstering her courage. And then her courage vanished as their bell rang. Not the distant one for breakfast, but the one on the edge of their property.

The elders were there, as promised, with their last task.

She and Carner exchanged a glance, stepping outside.

After giving sufficient warning with the bell and waiting a while, two elders entered the clearing. "Talia. Carner." They eyed the couple. "No marks." Looks of disapproval settled into the aged creases of their faces. "We see you've completed the primary task of the home."

Talia and Carner nodded. Talia felt as small as a sprout.

"We'll inspect it." The elders walked inside while the pair stayed glued in place.

If you want me, just say something. She begged, pleaded with her heart. But Carner said nothing.

The elders returned, and one whistled loudly. "Very nice quality. It is a shame to be wasted because you could not grow together after this much time."

Her knees were weak, her stomach churning. They didn't understand everything she and Carner had been working through.

And then a few young boys stalked into the clearing, bales of straw over their shoulders.

An elder instructed the boys where they could drop the straw and then ordered them to leave. After the boys were out of earshot, the elder again faced the couple, pulling out a jar of fire matches, setting it at his feet in the sand. "Your final task, if you choose to fully reject your match, is to burn the home to the ground before breakfast in the morning."

Talia gasped.

"No!" Carner protested. "We just spent an *entire month* building this with care!"

"To the ground," the elder repeated, his voice firm.

"That's a waste of supplies and time," Talia said. Even if she and Carner couldn't work things out, this was wrong. Their parents had invested in this property ... just like they had invested in Talia and Carner.

The elders' gaze was piercing, unforgiving. "Hatanii is not taken lightly. Much preparation goes into it. The elders do not assign matches on a whim. Nor do your parents approve of them lightly. Let that lesson settle with you, that adults in such arrangements learn to find a way to come together."

Tears pricked at Talia's eyes.

"If you accept your match, you will have marks at breakfast. If not, there will be smoke in the skies." The elders turned and left.

Talia struggled to breathe, tears falling down her cheeks. This was unfair. They'd put in *so* much work. This task was nothing but punishment, spite, and shame.

As Talia stood in place, shocked, stunned, and dismayed … Carner surprised her. He strode for the straw, and slowly pulled out a handful of it.

"What are you doing?" she asked, her voice shaky.

"What we're supposed to do." His tone held an edge.

"We don't have to."

"Yes, we do."

She grabbed his wrist, stopping him from dropping a single piece of the straw at the base of the home. He met her gaze, his jaw set.

"No, we don't." She searched his eyes, her heart nearly beating out of her chest. "We could… We could make this work."

He straightened. "Why? Because you're sad to lose the house? Or because you don't want to face everyone in shame?"

Yes. And yes. And so much more. She didn't want to lose *him*.

She took the straw from his hands. "Tell me you could never love me. That when you taunted me, it wasn't actually flirting."

He pursed his lips, his nostrils flared. "I made you feel horrible for years. I'm not a worthy match."

"I've forgiven you. Why are you acting like this?"

His eyes darted, searching, his mind working. "I… I don't…" He struggled to explain himself, as though he wasn't sure of his own answer.

"I have pride, too, Tali." Hurt was etched into every word. "How do you think it has felt for me this entire month? When you contested this, you pointed at me and said, 'This is a mistake.' Not that the match was. Me. *I* was the mistake." He yanked his hand free, reaching for something in the pocket of his shorts. "I spent *days* making this design for you." He pulled out the necklace she'd chucked into the ocean.

He'd found it…

"I watched you throw it," he confessed, his throat bobbing. "How do you think that has made me feel? When you said you would never forgive our parents for the match? You only gave hate. And I know I caused that, but…" He shook his head.

Her eyes shifted to the necklace again, and to the one he still wore that she'd made for him. She'd been abysmally cruel. And he'd been … sweet at times, fun at others, and yet cold and angry sometimes.

He had hurt her years ago without ever realizing it. And she'd just done the same to him. What person would want a partner who had constantly put them down without explanation?

"You only contested the match because I did," she said, guilt washing over her. The look of shock and disappointment he'd given at the reveal had possibly only been shock… And if she had been wearing his sandals that day, she too would have contested the match after he did. No one wanted to be in a loveless union where the other failed to give them a moment of consideration.

A longing stare was all the answer she received.

"I'm sorry," she choked out. They had both made mistakes. He had tried time and time again to befriend her, to right things, but he hadn't spoken up for himself, at least not enough for her to get the message.

They had been matched. She had finally made space in her heart and future for him. The magik of the window proved that this match hadn't been a failure. But had they ruined their opportunity?

She had felt at home in his arms just hours ago. As her mind drifted there, she recalled their first night together and the things they'd said. "You told me you wouldn't touch me even if I asked you to." Her heart was racing, her breathing heavy. "I'm asking you to. I want you to kiss me, Carner."

His breathing shuddered, and he took a step forward, a hand sliding to hold the nape of her neck. He bent and pressed his soft lips to hers, savoring a kiss that lit her heart aflame.

Every ounce of her hesitancy wilted away. She became undone.

One kiss turned into ten, his fingers digging into her hair, his other hand on her waist, her arms around his neck. It was dizzying, intoxicating, and unifying.

He leaned his forehead against hers, panting. "I have *always* loved you, Tali. Always."

Love was such a strong word, but if a first kiss could give her the kind of passion that made her knees almost buckle, and if their friendship had truly been reinstated…

They gazed into each other's eyes as she gathered her breath, not sure how to answer. Not wanting to say the wrong thing this time. And they had less than a day to make a final decision. There was so much pressure behind that decision. This was a lifelong commitment, not to be taken lightly. If she accepted him, and he her, he would be the father of her children someday.

She had held on to her pain for too long, and held equal blame in this hatanii going wrong. Throughout this entire process, even when she'd been wickedly cruel, he had been kind, and had never intentionally made her feel less than she was. He really wasn't that boy anymore. Her heart felt … safe.

"I love you, too," she whispered.

He did not wait for her to ask for another kiss, and this one was twice as passionate as the first. Time may very well have stopped. It was just the two of them in that moment—not a bird in the sky, not another soul on that island—as the magik did its work in their hearts.

Eventually, they had to come up for air. "I love you," he repeated. "Can I…" He bent, picking up the necklace he'd abandoned in their passion. "Can I give this back to you?"

She pulled her hair to the side and smiled as he strung it around her neck. "Does this mean…?" she started. *Less than twenty-four hours.* Matching soulmate marks, or smoke in the sky. But what if they chose neither? Their society was unforgiving. Families and friends would be disappointed. Akaii could probably date and marry, but she genuinely didn't know where they lived or how their families worked.

And the fact was, she did love Carner. She did want this house, and the blessings of hatanii, and the blessings it would bring upon their children someday. And he was a good man. Flawed, as was she. But good. He had goals, and talents, and a heart of gold.

Carner didn't ask, studying her as she worked through it. "I promise to do everything I can to make you happy, Tali. To be a good partner."

She was nervous. "We've only just kissed…" It was the kind of kiss that could easily lead to other things, but she was still scared. And then something in her calmed. He'd been hesitant about the idea of trying to be friends after returning to their respective islands as akaii. She now understood why. She couldn't imagine being *just* friends anymore.

Her mother's words of wisdom rang in her ears. *Keep an open mind. Trust the process. Treasure the experience.*

"We have all day and night," he said. "We don't have to rush. We… We could start by going inside…" He gently stroked her cheek, his perfect lips turned up. "And we can see how the last of our gifts look in our home."

The decorations. Our home. With each word from his lips, with each decision before her, the magik of the match etched into her heart like the gold embedded in the crystal family window they'd created together.

He leaned forward and gave her the most tender kiss. Not on the lips, or the forehead, or the cheek. But on her temple. A question. A plea. Would she accept the mark? Would she accept the hatanii? Would she accept him as he was?

"Yes."

Epilogue

The bonfire blazed brightly, the music performance enriching the celebration. Talia leaned into Carner, her hatanii mark resting against his shoulder. She couldn't keep a smile from her face. He drew lazy circles on her other shoulder, and they watched as dancers performed an elegant routine with their magik.

Talia and Carner had taken their time on that last day. She still resented the elders to a degree, and society as a whole, for pressing them to rush their decision, but perhaps that was the last push Talia and Carner had truly needed. And she only resented them as much as she did herself and Carner. If he had been more open about his feelings for her, about his desires, about how she'd made him feel, they wouldn't have wasted so much time. If she had opened up and swallowed her pride sooner, they may have enjoyed the month-long seclusion of hatanii a lot more.

But the past was the past. The mistakes of their childhood, and even their adulthood. They'd have chances to make new mistakes. A lifetime of chances.

She shifted on the couple's bench, and Carner caught her gaze. His eyes and smile were so mesmerizing. And that look… That look lit a fire in her. He was her soulmate—a complement to her temperament, education, and magik.

"Stop looking at me like that," she whispered. His lips quirked further up. It *wasn't* a sneer. It was the smile of an old childhood friend once lost, the smile of a lover.

He leaned his head down, pressing his lips to her ear. "I will *always* look at you like this, so you shouldn't glance my way when you don't want to see me adoring you."

Across the firepit, one of the other hatanii brides spied Carner leaning in, and gave Talia a happy, knowing look. They hadn't shared with a single soul what had happened, that they'd contested the match, fought it tooth and nail. No one needed to know that for now.

They hadn't told their parents after the morning's breakfast earlier in the day, as they'd greeted them from the ferry. Their parents had been so happy for them, and it had only made Talia happier.

She loved Carner. If society and tradition and even their families melted away from the scope of her consideration, she'd still choose him now, every time. Perhaps someday they'd share details of the botched ceremony with their children, so they'd learn from the lesson. But for now, they were content to enjoy pure bliss with each other.

Stars winked in the dark night sky as the celebration ceremony continued, Talia and Carner's parents flanking the couple. The morning's greeting ceremony had been much more private and casual. They'd given their parents a tour of the property, the finished home. *Their* home, adorned with the gifts they'd made for each other. The wards on the property had been lifted, and their parents had blessed the union.

Soon, the new couple would ferry their childhood belongings to their new home, and find their place with employment. They'd already discussed their future together, and every single part of it was an exciting new adventure.

Talia rested a hand on Carner's knee, and he slipped his hand into hers. She was calm in her heart as she squeezed. With her other hand, she rubbed the pendant he'd made for her.

Sharing a bed as a wed couple, earning themselves matching soulmate marks, finishing a home together—these had never truly been the end goal. They'd opened a door.

For them, this was only the beginning.

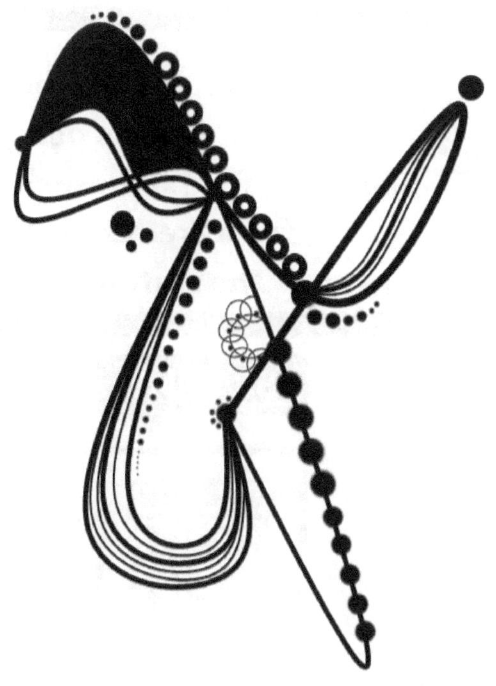

~Don't forget to leave a review!~

On Amazon, Goodreads, StoryGraph, and/or anywhere else this book can be found.

Want to read a few bonus scenes from Carner's perspective? Sign up for J. Houser's newsletter for a free download of *The Hatanii Groom*!

JHouserWrites.com

Also, connect with the author here:
On YouTube, TikTok, Facebook, Instagram, and Twitter under:
JHouserWrites

Other books by J. Houser

THE
SEEDER WARS TRILOGY   THE
HEIR'S DUOLOGY

Seeder Wars is a Young Adult Contemporary Romantic Fantasy series featuring unique magic, botanical beings, spies, & assassins. The series starts with a central trilogy and expands to a spin-off duology (& more on the way!)

Looking for an elegant and fun way to keep track of your reads?
Paper and Ink Trophies is a hardback book journal, easily disguised as another novel on your shelf! It includes entry pages for 500 books, as well as places to list your TBR, DNFs, and more!

About the Author

J. Houser grew up watching a ton of sci-fi with her dad, so fantasy and sci-fi have naturally become her preferred genres to write in. After living in Poland for a year and a half, she looked into their fairy tales and found the inspiration for this story. The Polynesian vibes are partially inspired by her adventures in New Zealand, Fiji, and Hawaii.